Family
Tradition

By

Herm Rawlings

ISBN: 9781092958967

Cover design by Traise Rawlings and John Sheirer.

Photos courtesy of the author.

https://scanticbooks.blogspot.com

Facebook: Scantic Books

—

Dedication

This effort is dedicated to two people. First, my wife Kim who first recognized my writing capabilities and has encouraged me endlessly to take the next step and stick with writing this book. Thank you for pushing me to achieve something I've always wanted to do. Believe me (and she knows), I'm not known for following through with a whole lot. Second, my son, Traise. His love and dedication to writing lit the flame for me to take a three-page, handwritten story that I wrote over thirty years ago while onboard the Coast Guard Cutter Tamaroa as part of a crew contest, and turn it into the following tale. It's wonderful when a son inspires his father, and you have done that many times. Thank you, both. At the end of my life, if I'm remembered simply as Kim's husband or Traise's dad, I'll be just fine with that. (By the way, I won that contest.)

One

This winter day in 1983 began like any other as the Tuckahoma, an unassuming Coast Guard cutter, sailed down the east coast with Seaman Josh Hartman on board in service to his country in the United States Coast Guard. The Tuckahoma left her home port of Portsmouth, New Hampshire, just twenty-four hours before and was making good time on the trip to her patrol area in the Caribbean for a scheduled ninety-day assignment to cruise the area on a drug interdiction mission.

Young Seaman Hartman and his crewmates welcomed this break from the harsh Northeast winter with the hope of enjoying some balmy conditions down south. They had lucked out because usually in mid-February, the seas some forty miles off the coast of North Carolina's Cape Hatteras were notoriously rough and made for a quite uncomfortable transit through the area until they reached the calmer waters of South Carolina. But on this day, the Atlantic was uncharacteristically calm. The Tuckahoma's well-worn but still very capable General Motors diesel engines hummed along and pushed the old girl through the glass-like ocean at a smooth six nautical miles per hour. No one on board could have suspected how soon their progress south would be interrupted.

* * *

The Tuckahoma had been a Navy ocean-going tugboat when commissioned in 1943, but when the service decided it no longer needed her, she was transferred to the U.S. Coast Guard to continue her life as a 205-foot cutter. Although she had begun to show her age, the crew of eighty-five enlisted men and eight officers worked hard to maintain her in top condition, both mechanically and in appearance. The constant painting and repainting of her interior and exterior, along with maintaining her engines, was a continuing pain in the butt—but the crew took it all in stride. She was their home away from home when underway, and they took great pride in the daily tasks that were required to keep her in the best shape possible. It was as if their lives depended on her—and, in fact, they did.

Josh had been on board the ship for eight months. This was his third patrol but the first going south. The previous patrols had taken place in the chilly North Atlantic on fishery patrol, so this voyage south was a welcome change.

He was scheduled for the 08:00 to 12:00 morning watch on the helm, so he had gotten up earlier than the rest of the crew to beat the rush to the showers. When the ship was underway, there was no long, hot, fifteen-minute, enjoyable, take-your-time-to-wake-up, spa-type of shower. The amount of water on board was extremely limited, so crew members had to indulge in a "sea shower." Basically, get in, turn the water on, get wet, turn the water off, soap up, turn the water back on, rinse, and then it's done. Quick but effective. But anyone caught being a "shower hog" and staying longer than necessary would incur the wrath of either the Master of Arms or the next guy in line, standing outside, wearing only his towel and flip-flops, ready to apply said flip-flops roughly to the offender's backside.

When Josh finished showering, combing his hair, and brushing his teeth, he exited the head and made his way back to his rack where he dressed in his work uniform—the same clothes he had worn for the past three days. He didn't get to do laundry that often while underway, so he had to stretch out the usage for as many wearings as possible. As long as they didn't stink too much or were stained, they were good to go.

Josh quietly made his way through the berthing area, passing many sleeping shipmates, and went up the ladder to the chow line for breakfast. The chow line always opened at 06:00 and ran until 08:00. He grabbed a hard, plastic tray from the stack at the head of the line and slid it down the rail to where the cook was patiently waiting to take his order. Each morning, the menu was basically the same, with scrambled eggs, bacon, sausage, and fruit available for the crew. Crew members could also have eggs to order—as long as the cook on duty was in a good mood and the weather wasn't too bad. If the ship was rocking and rolling, there was no way the cooks could keep a cracked egg within the confines of the flat-top grill.

Since the sea was pleasant and calm this morning, Josh placed his order for a couple "dippy eggs." The Subsistence Specialist First Class (known as the SS1) always teased him about that name. When he was growing up in Southwestern Pennsylvania, that's what the young sailor called eggs over easy or sunny side up. The SS1 had never heard the term before, and when Josh ordered them the first time, the specialist just looked at him and said, "You want what?" The ritual conversation had become a friendly tease ever since.

Having obtained his "dippy eggs"

and the rest of his breakfast, Josh walked the short passageway to the mess deck and took a seat next to Dave Saggett, the Damage Controlman Second Class (DC2) who had arrived a few minutes earlier. They had become quick friends after Josh reported aboard, mostly because their racks were directly across from each other in the same berthing cubicle. Crew members couldn't help but get to know and converse with someone when they lived just a few feet apart day in and day out.

Because of the good weather, the watertight hatches on both sides of the mess deck had been latched open, which allowed a warm breeze to flow across the mess deck.

"What a great morning," said Dave.

"A hell of a lot better than what we left back home, huh?" Josh chuckled.

"Got that right," the DC2 replied. "I imagine the wives are back home cussing us right now while they're digging out from all the snow."

Josh had a fleeting thought of his new wife Annie, who waited at home for him, but he pushed it out of his mind for the moment.

They both finished up the morning meal and headed to the fantail for morning muster. Except for those crewmembers on watch, everyone had to gather by division for the day's news from the Executive Officer, assignments from the department heads, and to ensure that all were physically accounted for.

Following muster, Josh grabbed a cup of coffee (otherwise affectionately known as "sludge") from the mess deck and headed to the bridge for his four-hour watch, which consisted of one hour manning the helm, switching with the lookout for the next hour, back to the helm, and finally finishing back up on the lookout perch.

Upon arrival, Josh found the usual cast of characters. The Officer of the Deck (OOD), Radarman (RD), Quartermaster (QM), Boatswain Mate of the Watch (BMOW), and Helmsman getting ready to stand down and hand the ship over to the next watch. The young man who was manning the helm looked at him and provided the current course to maintain, and then offered Josh the helm, stating in the formal military tone of a trained seaman, "On the Bridge, Helmsman stands relieved."

Josh grabbed the large wooden wheel, repeated the course, and reciprocated with similar military discipline, "I have assumed the helm. Steering one-eight-zero degrees." The only deviation of the routine would be if orders were given by the OOD to change course or if Josh had to make a quick trip to the head. He had yet to learn never to drink coffee prior to going on watch.

During the early part of his watch, the ship came to life with all the crewmembers performing their usual daily tasks while underway. The engineers were in the engine room doing preventive maintenance on the equipment that kept the old ship up and running. Deck force personnel were out and about, chipping the ever-evolving rusty paint from the metal portions of the ship or cleaning and maintaining the exterior deck that was covered in non-slip paint. The mess cooks were sweeping and swabbing the mess deck, cleaning up from breakfast, and starting to set up for the noon meal. Everything was just as it should be, and no one had any idea of what was about to happen within the next twenty-four hours.

Two

Josh had joined the Coast Guard right out of high school—against his mother's wishes. She had lost her husband, Josh's father, Navy Lieutenant David Hartman, when Josh was just six years old in 1970. The officer had been lost at sea when the Navy supply ship he was assigned to left its home port of Norfolk, Virginia, on a routine cruise and mysteriously disappeared. A thirty-day search by the Navy and Coast Guard found no trace of the ship or crew after communications were lost three days into the trip. This was the second member of Josh's family who had been tragically lost at sea. His Grandfather, Samuel Hartman, a Navy Chief Boatswains Mate, mysteriously disappeared while on leave and fishing by himself on his twenty-four-foot Boston Whaler off the coast of Florida way back in 1952.

From a young age, the details surrounding his father's death were forever embedded in Josh's mind. He couldn't forget the look on his mother's face as the Navy Chaplain arrived on their doorstep and explained that her husband's ship was lost at sea with no survivors. The tears his mother wept as she told him that Daddy wouldn't be coming home were always just a memory away.

Josh's mother never remarried, and although it was tough, she managed to work two jobs and raise her only son to become a thoughtful and respectable young man who never shied away from any challenge. He was always silently jealous of the other boys in school, seeing them and their dads working on cars, playing catch, going fishing, and all the other things that fathers and sons did together. Throughout his young life, he had felt cheated that he never had the chance to know his dad like they knew theirs. The toughest times were always around the holidays and special days, Thanksgiving, Christmas, Father's Day, birthdays—but even ordinary school events and routine moments always had something missing ... his dad.

Ever since he could remember, Josh loved being around the water. After his dad died, he and his mom moved to her hometown of Hyndman, Pennsylvania, a small and sleepy landlocked town just across the state line north of Cumberland, Maryland. Even then, he always spent his summers either on Shawnee

Lake or hanging with friends swimming in the waters of Gooseberry Creek, jumping off the railroad bridge into what was called "The Pitt" or one of the other hometown swimming holes that were peppered throughout the area. Although he had never been to the Atlantic Ocean just a few hundred miles away, he constantly felt the pull of the sea.

When the time came after graduation, Josh knew what he had to do. It took a lot of thought and even more talking to his mother, who he hated to leave, but the decision was made. He enlisted in the Coast Guard. He had looked into the Air Force and the Navy but the Coast Guard was a much smaller military service. He figured he wouldn't feel like just another number in the big picture—plus he would probably be stationed somewhere in the states because the Coast Guard doesn't have many overseas assignments.

Even if he went to the West Coast, he would still only be a plane flight away from his darling Annie. To him, it was a no-brainer. He was going where he had to go, a place where he could not only help people who needed him but also where his heart said he had to be. The ocean was a place he had never been, but deep in his soul, Josh felt the open water was meant to be his home.

He left Hyndman in June of 1982 on a bus that took him to the Coast Guard Training Center in Cape May, New Jersey. He had never been away from home for more than a week or so during summer camps, so what awaited him was quite a shock. The first few weeks were tough. The constant stress of being yelled at, told when and how to eat, when to sleep, when to get up, how to make your bed, the constant marching drills and extreme physical activity—it was almost too much to bear. The purpose of Basic

Training is to break you down to your lowest level and then gradually build you back up with the knowledge, confidence, and instincts that would be required to handle any type of situation that may be presented during your career. He dealt initially with a severe bout of homesickness and had actually thought about quitting and going back home.

One evening, after a particularly tough day, Josh found himself outside the office of his Company Commander, a hard-nosed, short BM1 with the nickname, "The Rooster." The name and description matched his personality "to a T" because whenever The Rooster got mad, his angry gait and high-pitched voice duplicated the mad, wet, male member of the poultry family. Josh was ready to knock on the office door and tell him that he had had enough of the constant mental and physical demands. He felt done and wanted to be released so he could return to Annie and the comforts and easy life that would be still waiting for him back home.

Before he could knock, Josh was suddenly surrounded by three other company commanders who were walking down the hallway. He was about to experience the dreaded "Wolfpack." The commanders of Tango, Uniform, and Victor companies all stood within inches of Josh and began interrogating him about why he was out of the barracks at this time of evening and in front of the Whiskey Company commander's office. The barrage was loud and unrelenting as his manhood, confidence, dedication, and even his overall purpose in life were addressed and questioned. They wanted him to quit— but then again, they didn't. This was a watershed moment in his life, and as the trio of hellcats disgustingly walked away, he lifted his hand to bang on the door, ready to end his short military experience.

With his fist in motion, halfway to the door, he stopped, paused for a few seconds, and then stood straight up as if coming to attention. "No," he said emphatically to himself. "This is not going to beat me. *I can do this*." And with a renewed sense of determination, he did an about-face and returned to the barracks. That was the last time Josh ever waivered. He knew that he would not, *he could not*, be denied his destiny.

With a new and clear focus, the remaining weeks of boot camp were not exactly easier, but there was light at the end of the tunnel. Josh would go on to graduate with honors and, during the final week, receive his orders. The week before, all future graduates had been given the chance to choose up to five Coast Guard units (either shore-based or underway) where they would like to be assigned. Most new graduates almost always picked shore-based locations geographically close to their homes—but not Josh. All five of his choices were for Coast Guard Cutters far away from Southwest Pennsylvania. Two were based in Florida, one in North Carolina, one in Virginia, and one in Texas

When the time came, he was surprised to find out that he had been assigned to the Coast Guard Cutter Tuckahoma, based out of Portsmouth, New Hampshire. Not on the list of his preferred units, this cutter was one of the oldest ships in the fleet. She was an ocean-going tug boat with a notorious reputation as the service's only "submarine." The moniker was jokingly attached to the ship a few years earlier when a disgruntled and drunken crewman had returned to the ship from a night out and opened the bilges, allowing sea water to rush into the engine room. While moored to the dock, the ship had sunk up to its main deck. Although having experienced heavy water damage throughout, she was a tough old bird. Following a much-heralded salvage operation, "The Mighty Tuck" returned to duty and continued her long life as one of the most dependable cutters in the Coast Guard.

With excitement, the young Josh accepted the orders (as if he had a choice) and, along with his fellow graduates, left the confines of Training Center Cape May with full sea bags and orders in hand. Josh headed back to Hyndman, excited to see Annie, then still his fiancé, for a few weeks. He decided to ask her a very important question upon his return, and he really hoped her answer would be yes. It was.

Annie had been his high school sweetheart going back years, and she gleefully accepted his surprise proposal while he was home after boot camp. They hadn't told anyone when they went to the local courthouse and got married. They managed to keep it secret since then, but they planned to have a formal wedding when he returned from this patrol.

His future was now set, and there was no looking back. But Josh would soon learn the strange fact that sometimes a personal vision of destiny and the reality of fate can be dramatically different from each other.

Three

At the end of Josh's time on the helm watch, fresh crewmembers arrived and the process of switching out took place. Josh turned over the helm, exited the bridge, and headed down to the lower decks. He made his way back to the mess deck and chow line for the afternoon meal, which was always an adventure. He was constantly amazed at the ability of the cooks to take whatever was left over from breakfast and incorporate it into the next meal. As he inspected the layout before him, he had to chuckle when he noticed that the morning's scrambled eggs had become an ingredient in the fried rice while the leftover sausage had been cut in small chunks and was now making an appearance in the chili. Josh didn't want to imagine what might be in the meatloaf, so a ham sandwich and chili it was.

The mess deck was almost always full for lunch, and sometimes Josh had to wait a minute or two to get a seat. But today he spied an opening next to the Doc, the Hospital Corpsman First Class (HS1) and quickly made his way over to sit down next to him. The medic had a first name but not many onboard, including Josh, knew what it was. He was just "Doc." The only medical person onboard, Doc was responsible for the health and well-being of the entire crew. If any crew members got sick or got injured, Doc was always there to treat them and get them back into service. One of the first things Josh learned when reporting onboard his first ship was that there were two people (other than the Captain) that you never pissed off. One was the cook and the other was Doc. Both could make your life miserable if you fell on the wrong side of them, and both could provide comfort on the long voyages, be that comfort food from the cooks or medical care from Doc. Needless to say, Doc had a lot of friends.

"Have a seat, Boot," Doc said to the youngster. "Boot" was the automatic name given to every Coastie right out of boot camp. Whether you liked it or not, you were "Boot" until the next new, fresh-faced junior sailor out of Cape May arrived.

"What's the topic for today?" Doc asked in his always friendly manner.

"Not sure, Doc," Josh replied. "I just got off watch. How 'bout yourself?"

Doc took a sip from his cup of "bug juice" (Kool-aid to the outside world).

"Just another day in paradise here on the ocean of life," he mused. "I'm loving the hell out of this weather, though. May have to go topside for a bit and catch some rays."

Doc didn't have to stand watches underway and pretty much had the run of the ship. Being on call twenty-four hours a day and taking care of everybody earned him the right to do what he wanted and go where he needed to be. It wasn't uncommon to find Doc in the Chief's Quarters playing Spades or Hearts with the crews' senior enlisted members.

Doc turned slightly serious for a moment. "Heard that we're about to go through the Bermuda Triangle in a few hours. How ya feel about that?"

The young sailor shrugged his shoulders. "Haven't really thought about it. Don't think there's much to all that anyway."

Doc gave a short laugh. "Yeah, me

either. But if you listen to some of these guys on here, you'd think we were getting ready to sail into the oblivion or something. I think they've watched a few too many episodes of *In Search Of.*"

Doc finished up his meal, wiped his mouth and stood up. "Well, that's it for me. It's a wonder we don't all lose weight eating this crap. If you need me after that attempt of a so-called meal, you know where to find me."

Josh smiled and nodded his head. "See ya, Doc."

After finishing his lunch, Josh decided to head out to the fantail (the rear of the ship) and check out what was going on there. Some crewmembers were fishing while others were reading or just lying around with their shirts off grabbing some sunshine. One was even attempting to fly a homemade kite. If Josh squinted his eyes, he could almost imagine this as a normal day back home at Shawnee Lake.

Life is pretty good, Josh thought as he sat down and looked out over the vast ocean. Not a cloud in the sky, warm temperatures, and the sea was smooth. "This is what I was looking for," he said to himself as he slowly nodded off. "Yep, pretty damn good."

The remainder of the day was non-eventful. After his brief siesta on the fantail, he hung out with the other junior sailors in the berthing area, listening to music, playing cards, and basically shooting the breeze until the evening meal. Then it was only a short time before he had to go back on watch for another four hours from 20:00 to 24:00 hours. Then he'd hit the rack to sleep before his next shift.

This was the same routine for each day while underway. Eat, stand watch, conduct emergency drills, slap some paint on a bulkhead somewhere, sleep, eat again, screw around, stand watch, go to bed, and prepare to do the same thing the next day. Lather, rinse, re-peat—sometimes leisurely, sometimes as quick as a sea shower. But always predicable, orderly, ordinary.

This time, though, the next day would be anything but ordinary.

Four

Josh made his way up to the bridge to begin his 20:00 to 24:00 watch. All was fairly quiet and relaxed as each watch stander passed along information the new crew needed to maintain the ship's course, speed, engine status, and such. As they had done on every previous watch, Josh and his watch partner, Seaman Kyle Jacobs, flipped a coin to determine who would man the helm first and who would head to the lookout position. At the end of each hour, the two would rotate jobs, with each taking turns as the "driver" of the ship using the huge wooden wheel that looked like it belonged on a pirate ship to maintain the ship's course.

Kyle called "heads" as Josh tossed a quarter into the air, caught it on the way down with one hand, and slapped the coin on the back of his other hand to reveal the findings. Seeing that heads was showing, Kyle stated that he'd take the helm first, so Josh headed out onto the bridgewing and up the ladder to the lookout platform to begin the first hour of the four-hour stint.

After sailing non-stop for almost two days, the ship was now off the coast of Florida. Josh welcomed the warm breeze and clear sky as he no longer had to bundle up as he did while up north. Long underwear and a parka gave way to uniform shorts and a blue Tuckahoma T-shirt. The lookout portion of the watch was actually quite relaxing. After doing a 360-degree scan of the sea with his binoculars every few minutes, Josh would lean against the steel and plexiglass wind break and just enjoy his surroundings. For a while, Josh wondered if his father and grandfather had ever stood watch like this as young sailors. Of course they had, he realized. All young sailors stood watch in some form when onboard a ship. It was a rite of passage.

Josh reached into his pocket and pulled out a folded sheet of paper. He didn't even need to unfold it because he had read it so many times during the past four days. He just caressed it between his thumb and index finger, imagining the paper was the soft skin of his new wife, Annie. She slipped the one-page note to him as they kissed goodbye on the pier before he boarded for this long patrol.

In the note, Annie told him not only how much she loved him, but also how proud she was of him, how happy she was to be his wife, and that she was so excited to share the rest of their lives together. The last line of the note perplexed him, though. Annie had written that when he got home, she had a surprise for him. Pondering that surprise kept his mind going during the long hours of many shifts on board the Tuckahoma.

Other than an oil tanker or cruise ship in the distance, nothing much seemed worth noticing during his watch. For just a moment, Josh thought he saw a peculiar area on the horizon, but when he tried to focus his eyes on it through the binoculars, nothing was there. The sea can play tricks on the eyes, Josh knew. He let his mind drift back to thoughts of Annie and the excitement of seeing her again and discovering the surprise that she would reveal.

At the end of the first hour of watch,

Josh and Kyle switched out and then repeated the ritual two more times until the new watch crew reported to the bridge and relieved them of the watch. Josh was happy to see that his friend, Ron Drummond, a big, no-nonsense, country kid from Montana, was on the relief crew that night. Montana might be far from Josh's native Pennsylvania, but the two men shared a similar dedication to their duty. Josh knew that the ship was in good hands with the steady Drummond at lookout.

Returning to the berthing area just after midnight, Josh undressed, hung his uniform on the pole attached to the bunk and hopped into his rack, situated in the middle of the three-tiered sleeping quarters. The small space didn't allow much comfort as he had to lie on his stomach or back. If Josh attempted to sleep on his side, his shoulder would actually touch the bottom of the rack above him. Josh got situated and pulled the curtain closed that offered at least a small amount of privacy. Then he drifted off into a well-deserved sleep.

* * *

At 02:00 on the bridge, the mid-watch Officer of the Deck, Ensign Chad Thomas, examined the navigational chart on the Quartermaster's table, ensuring they were still on course. Suddenly, Drummond's voice boomed from the lookout's voice pipe, startling Thomas. "Lookout to Bridge!"

Recovering from the surprise and regaining his usual calm demeanor, Ensign Thomas walked over to the voice pipe casually and put his mouth close to the opening. "Bridge. What's wrong? You bored up there?"

Drummond came back, "No, sir. Just checking if you're seeing anything on the radar directly ahead of us."

Thomas looked at the Radarman with a raised eyebrow. "Well? Are we?"

The Radarman took a quick glance at his screen and said, "Nothing showing up, sir. No contacts or weather fronts anywhere around us."

Thomas again spoke into the voice pipe. "We're not showing anything here. You got something up there?"

Drummond's voice retuned through the pipe. "Not sure, sir. Just something ... something weird on the horizon." His voice formed a question even though his words were a statement. "There's a weird area where I can't see the difference between the ocean and the sky."

The OOD looked around to the others on the bridge, shook his head, and directed his words back to the lookout. "You want to explain that to me, please?"

"It's just weird, sir," Drummond replied, something unsure in his usually steady voice. "I'm looking around up here, and there's nothing but clear skies with stars all over the place and moonlight. But in the distance, there's an area ahead of us that's just totally black. I can't tell where the ocean stops and the sky begins, and there's no stars whatsoever."

The QM laughed and said, "He didn't eat the chili tonight, did he, sir?"

The OOD grinned and responded into the voice pipe again. "Well, just keep an eye on it, and let me know if anything changes."

"Aye aye, Bridge. Will do." Drummond hesitated for a moment and then continued, "It does seem to be coming our way pretty quick, though."

The RD looked into his screen again and reported to Thomas, "I still have nothing, sir, but I'll continue to monitor."

Ensign Thomas lowered his head

and said to himself, but loud enough for everyone on the bridge to hear, "Just what I need. A lookout that needs a piss test."

* * *

Above the bridge at his station, Drummond continued to scan the horizon around the ship, but he always came back to that strange black area straight ahead. It was definitely getting larger and closer, but he hesitated to report what he was seeing to the Bridge. He figured it must be some type of atmospheric anomaly since the OOD said there was nothing on the radar. Whatever it was, the only word he could use to describe it was "weird." It was like nothing he had ever observed before. Nothing about herding cattle and building fences as a teenager in land-locked Montana had prepared him for what he saw out across the ocean. He did notice that the wind had picked up a bit, but he'd been at sea long enough to know that wasn't totally unusual for this area of the Atlantic at night.

Drummond let the words "Bermuda Triangle" float to the surface of his mind, but then he pushed them back down. He wasn't going to let ghost stories get in the way of doing his duty. He was just glad he had just one more hour or so on watch so he could get some sleep and not have to worry about mysterious dark voids in the night.

* * *

Back on the Bridge, the QM looked at the weather instruments and noticed the wind gaining speed. "Mr. Thomas, wind is increasing to ten knots, but I can't determine the direction."

Ensign Thomas acknowledged the report with a nod of his head. "Something wrong with the wind indicator?" he asked.

The QM tapped on the gauge a few times with his fingernail. "Possibly. The needle is going back and forth from east to west instead of staying in one direction."

The Ensign walked over to the QM station and tapped on the indicator himself with the same result. "Make sure we get that checked out first thing in the morning."

"Mr. Thomas!" a voice rang out.

Thomas quickly turned toward the shout and saw Ron Drummond standing on the bridge with eyes wide open and a look of terror on his face.

"What are you doing down—"

Before Thomas could finish his question, Drummond blurted. *"Sir, it's right on top of us!"*

Suddenly, only the glow of the nighttime red lights illuminated the bridge as the bright moonlight that had been shining through the windows all night disappeared.

Drummond and the bridge crew became eerily quiet as the radios went silent, and the radar screens began to flicker. The needle on the large magnetic compass started spinning, and the men could feel the temperature dropping dramatically. Every bridge crew member stopped what they were doing and looked at each other in confusion.

"What the hell's going on?" Thomas muttered under his breath.

After a few seconds, without warning, the ship pitched violently upwards. Oversized waves began to hit the ship from all directions as the bridge crew struggled to keep their footing. They held onto anything they could find to keep themselves upright. Just a minute before, the seas had been calm. But now the cutter was floundering and pitching in thirty-foot waves with tons of angry seawater attacking her. Within half a minute, the Captain was on the bridge.

"Secure all exterior hatches *now*!" the Captain commanded with authority. The bridge crew didn't need to look to know that the booming voice came from their highly respected Captain, Commander Ezekiel Dillon. "Captain Zeke" was a slightly rotund twenty-five-year veteran of the Coast Guard on his third stint as a ship's commanding officer. His reputation and authority were non-negotiable and well earned. He looked sternly at Ensign Thomas. "Why wasn't I notified of this incoming weather?"

The Ensign staggered toward the Captain, trying to keep his balance and his voice calm and professional despite the panic-inducing situation. "Captain, we had no indications there was anything at all out here. One second it was calm, and the next we were taking waves over the bow. Nothing on radar and no advisories were received over the radio. It popped up out of nowhere."

The Captain wasn't sure he could believe what he was hearing. In all his years of underway time while in the Coast Guard, he had never had a storm of this size "just pop up."

As he and the rest of the bridge crew were trying to maintain their balance during the sudden onslaught of weather and high seas, the QM shouted out, *"Captain! Starboard side!"*

The Captain turned and was stunned at what he was looking at. Even in the darkness surrounding the ship, the Captain could see the white-cap of a huge wall of water at least eighty feet high as it hurdled towards the ship. Without hesitation, he commanded, *"Sound general quarters and brace for impact!"*

Before the Quartermaster could sound the alarm, the massive wave slammed into the cutter with such force that it pushed the nearly two-thousand-ton ship over until she was almost entirely on her left side. Water poured down the Tuckahoma's stacks, flooding the engine room and shorting out the electrical systems. The old girl had never had to endure a roll of this magnitude and degree before, and no one could predict if she could recover. Surprised watch standers throughout the ship were flung around like rag dolls. Those not on duty were sleeping in their beds. They were suddenly and violently thrown from the racks, landing on each other or slammed against lockers.

The old ship remained on its port side for what seemed like an eternity. It was as if she was deciding whether to fight or accept her fate and continue to roll over completely and head to the sea floor, taking her loyal crew with her. Slowly, ever so slowly, the old girl began to shift back towards starboard until she was upright once again. Although still being pounded with the rough seas, she had survived the forty-five-degree roll—but just barely.

"Sound that alarm now and get me a damage report!" the Captain bellowed as he picked himself off the deck of the bridge. He looked around and saw the bridge crew slowly getting to their feet. The QM grabbed the ship's microphone while pulling the GQ alarm switch. "Now general quarters! General quarters! *All hands man your GQ stations!"*

The Captain glanced quickly at each of the bridge crew and saw that the helmsman was clutching his left arm, which appeared to have been broken when he collided with the bulkhead. "Quartermaster, man the helm! Ensign Thomas, get Doc up here if he's able!"

As the crew below and on the bridge began to recover, the Tuckahoma stabilized as best she could while still being pummeled with wave after wave. The ship's emergency lights had come on, but they would only last an hour or so. The Captain called out each of the bridge crew by their job title to make sure they were all okay and to get the current status of the ship. When he got to the Radarman, the RD showed a dazed but concerned look on his face. He then pointed towards the starboard windows and yelled, "Captain!"

The Commanding Officer glanced over his shoulder and then spun his entire body towards the starboard bridge wing. Through the soaked windows of the bridge, he saw another gigantic wave, even larger than the one they just barely survived, rapidly approaching. The Captain stood stoically, grabbed the closest brass handle mounted on the bulkheads around the bridge and muttered, "God help us all."

* * *

Down in the berthing area, crew-members were picking themselves up after being tossed out of their racks like an old Pop Goes the Weasel toy that had been wound too tightly. Most had been sleeping, but others had been reading or had their headphones on listening to music with their portable cassette players. Josh had been sleeping comfortably when the first monster wave hit. Even though the loud crash and sudden list of the ship startled him, his reflexes took over and he grabbed the side of his rack, holding on and preventing himself from being ejected out of the tight sleeping area. As the ship recovered and slowly righted itself, Josh and his shipmates began to scramble down, pull on their uniforms, and get to their assigned GQ stations. No one was sure what was going on—only that they had gone from a comfortable, somewhat peaceful sleep to total chaos in a matter of seconds.

Because of the crew's training, the entire berthing area had cleared out in an almost impossibly quick span of time with the exception of a few slightly injured crew members who were a bit slower than the rest. Josh's GQ assignment was located in the Aft Steering Compartment, a small interior space located close to the berthing area but still deep within the ship at the stern. This is where the ship's rudder could be manually controlled if the bridge lost steering control.

After quickly donning his uniform and stepping over a multitude of loose debris on the deck, Josh arrived at the hatch to Aft Steering and quickly undid the six latches on the metal door to the compartment and half stepped, half fell inside. Once in, he secured the hatch and hurriedly opened the metal box containing the sound-powered phones to set up communication with the bridge.

As he unwound the cord to plug into the ship's internal phone system, the second enormous wave hit.

With the second sudden and massive jolt to the ship, Josh instinctively attempted to grab one of the pipes attached to the bulkhead and hold on as the ship again heaved over. Before he could establish a firm grip, the force of the impact jerked his hand from the pipe and sent him smashing into the far bulkhead of the stern, hitting his head on the thick, cold steel and causing blackness to come over him ...

Five

Josh's vision came back first, blurry to begin with, but slowly refocusing until he could see clearly. Gradually, the fogginess in his head and uncomfortable confusion gave way to a feeling of eerie calmness. He had no idea how much time had passed since he was knocked out cold. The emergency lights of the tiny compartment had gone out, so the entire space was engulfed in compete darkness. The ship was no longer being tossed around, and the compartment was strangely silent.

Once he got his bearings, Josh slowly picked himself off the deck, being careful not to move too quickly until he was able to determine that he had no injuries. He was banged up a bit, but, overall, he survived and felt okay, except for the headache from the fall. He tugged on the six metal latches (known as "dogs" to the crew) which secured the watertight exit door and stepped out of the compartment. The sudden glow of the regular interior lighting made him cover his eyes and squint until his vision adjusted. He expected to see other crewmembers recuperating from the experience, but, instead, he saw no one and heard only the low groan of the ship's engines.

Even though he was still a bit woozy, he automatically secured the door from the outside and gingerly made his way through the small passageway, glancing into the crew's head as he passed, expecting to see a stunned crewmember or two recovering the same way he was. But no one was there either. What he did notice was that the entire area wasn't covered in the clothes, books, trash, and other material that had been all over the deck and that he had to step over when he traversed to Aft Steering previously. In fact, there was no sign of the carnage from what they had endured anywhere.

The passageway opened into the ship's Aft Berthing where the First Class Petty Officers had a separate sleeping area on the left, and junior members had a larger area on the right. He glanced around and noticed that the junior area was unoccupied. No one was cleaning up from the storm or lying in the racks. All the bunks appeared to be made, and the entire area was spotless. Usually, there were at least a couple guys still in their racks after having the mid-watch from 24:00 until 04:00. They were allowed to stay in bed until 10:00, but not today. The First Class Quarters was just as deserted. Looking at his watch, he noted the time was 08:00. Josh couldn't figure out where the time had gone. *Strange*, he thought. *Maybe they're at muster topside.*

He continued through the forward berthing area. By habit (and training) turned right to climb the steep starboard ladder, which led to the main deck level of the ship. As with most Coast Guard ships' crew members, one of the first things Josh was taught upon returning to the boat was to transit up and towards the bow on the starboard side, and then down and towards the stern on the port side. This alleviated confusion and kept the passageways and ladders from being clogged with crewmen during times of an emergency. Everyone flowed in the same direction. Today, though, there were no other crewmen on the ladders.

At the top of the ladder, Josh proceeded up the starboard passageway, which passed the chow line. He now realized sunshine was coming through the open reinforced glass portholes. The light was somewhat of a welcomed sight to him after the dark night. Looking to his left into the galley, he noticed that, although deserted, the two large stainless steel vats used by the ship's cooks to make soups or stews were steaming as if they were just made, ready to have the ingredients added for the next meal. He walked past the drink line where the coffee pots were always brewing a batch of coffee and saw that both coffee stations had full containers with freshly brewed "sludge." The large plastic dispensers of "bug juice" were also both topped off.

Entering the mess deck, he saw a

dramatic absence of activity. Usually there was at least a junior mess cook around, either cleaning, setting up the tables with condiments, or just screwing off (which was usually the norm). But now? Nothing. He walked to the port side of the mess deck and glanced down the port passageway where the scullery was located. Some poor Seaman Apprentice earned his pay by working in this tiny, cramped space that contained the dishwashing machine, scrapping and cleaning all the food trays and utensils after a meal, plus all the pots and pans the cooks would stack up in the window. It was a hot, nasty, stinky job, but somebody had to do it. In fact, most were assigned to the job for only a week or two and then switched out with another junior member having the privilege for a while. But today, the scullery was silent and the trashcans were secured in place, emptied with new liners. Again, he saw no one.

"Okay, what the hell is going on?" Josh said aloud. He leaned out of both the port and starboard side hatches that were now opened, looking back and forth toward the bow and then the stern. As before, he saw no sign of anyone. A light ocean breeze was blowing through the open doorways and across the mess deck. This was the first time he noticed that the ship wasn't moving forward. The quad diesel engines were running—but were in neutral. The ocean was again calm and smooth as glass and gently rocked the ship, normal in these conditions.

A small bit of apprehension began to settle in Josh's stomach as he was slowly becoming confused about what was going on.

"There's eighty-five people on this ship and I can't find anyone? What the hell?" he said a bit louder, hoping there would be a return voice answering him from somewhere. But his voice and his hope went unanswered. He pushed through the mess deck door and started up the ladder to the next level. He stopped after a few steps and went back down the ladder that led down to Sickbay, Chief Quarters, the Electronic Shop, and other workspaces.

As he descended, he yelled out, "Anyone down there?" When he heard no response, he decided not to waste time and reversed direction up the ladder and headed toward the bridge. He passed the radio room on his way and noticed that the door to the classified space was wide open with no sign of the duty Radioman. A disturbing silence emitted from the space where, at any given time, day or night, and even with the door closed, you could hear voice transmissions, the teletype, or at least static from the radios. Now, nothing.

At the top of the ladder, Josh stepped onto the bridge and immediately was aware that it was, like the rest of the ship, deserted. No Officer of the Day barking commands at the helmsman, no Quartermaster or Radarman manning their stations, no Boatswain's Mate of the Watch present and, most importantly, no Captain. The sun was shining through the bridge windows, and the side bridge doors were latched open. A steaming cup of coffee sat in the cup holder of the Captain's chair and, at the Quartermaster's table, a lone pencil slowly rolled back and forth on the chart table surrounded by pieces of eraser shavings that are common on a working chart area.

All the electronics and radar screens were up and running, and the bridge radio systems were lit and active. It was as if everyone who should be there just up and walked off without a concern, leaving the entire bridge open and inviting the world in. Josh could feel confusion and even a bit of panic growing, and he struggled to push it down.

But where? his mind raced. *Where could they all have gone? Did they abandon ship?*

Josh reached up and grabbed a mic from one of the radios, ensured the dial was set to Channel 16 (the universal distress channel), squeezed it, and called out, "Mayday, Mayday. This is the Coast Guard Cutter Tuckahoma. If anyone can hear this transmission, please respond." He waited a few seconds for a reply. When none came through, he repeated his broadcast. Nothing but silence. He clipped the mic back on its holder, walked out to each bridge wing, looked back toward the stern on both sides, and found the small boats and inflatable raft containers still secured in their location.

Questions were consuming him at an ever-more-rapid pace as he made his way to the Captain's chair. Any other time, he wouldn't have even thought about touching the brass and leather throne of the Captain. No one sat in that chair except Captain Zeke, not even VIPs who toured the vessel. But he wasn't thinking rationally as he slowly pulled himself up onto the soft chair and stared out the bridge window, looking into a vast expanse of ocean. No land in site, no birds, no other ships. Nothing but a blue, cloudless sky, and an endless calm sea of uncertainty stared back at him.

Six

The seriousness of the situation hit Josh hard as he slumped in the Captain's chair, his mind going a thousand miles a minute. He lifted his head once more and peered out the window.

He suddenly felt the effects of being alone on the ship and reached back with his left hand and pulled his wallet out of his back pocket. Opening it, he took out two pictures that he always carried with him, the pictures that always helped him through tough times.

The first photo was of Annie. God, how he loved her. Even though the photo couldn't talk, just looking at her smile, long blonde hair, and dark green eyes conveyed the feeling of warmth and comfort he needed when life got a bit too hectic. Josh thought, *Don't worry Annie, we'll get through this, and I'll be home soon.*

He then looked at the second photo and peered into the eyes of his father, sharply dressed in the white uniform of a Navy Lieutenant, standing tall and proud, with his hands on the thin shoulders of his small son in front of him, ready to leave port on another mission that would take him from his family once again. He would never forget that day. It was the last time he ever saw his father.

He had felt it was his duty to carry out the work his father had begun. Now the irony of the situation hit him as he remembered his mother's reluctance when he wanted to go to sea. His father and grandfather had been lost in deep waters, and now he was looking at a seemingly similar fate, but with one major exception: he was still alive. But for how long?

Suddenly he heard something that jolted him back to reality, a barely audible low humming sound that he hadn't heard before.

"What the hell is that?" he said aloud, his voice echoing in the empty bridge.

Josh got out of the Captain's chair and walked out to the port side bridge wing to investigate the now louder-growing hum. Looking out over the bow, he could barely make out a few dots in the sky that were low on the horizon but appeared to be heading toward the ship. He quickly re-entered the bridge and grabbed a hanging pair of binoculars that were swinging back and forth with the gentle ocean and ran back to the port bridge wing and looked into the sky over the bow. In the distance, he saw the dots were actually five aircraft in formation heading right towards the ship. He couldn't make out the type, but that didn't make any difference. As long as they saw him, they could rescue him!

Josh ran to the chartroom, grabbed a pair of bright orange signal flags that were lying on a shelf, returned to the bridge wing, and jumped up the ladder to the flying bridge. There he began waving the flag back and forth over his head, hoping the planes that were approaching would see that he was in trouble.

The planes were still flying in a tight V-formation and coming straight at him, getting closer every second. He waited for some type of signal from them as they passed overhead just two hundred feet or so above the ship, but he saw no tip of the wings or any other type of acknowledgement.

As they receded in the sky, Josh realized that these planes didn't look like the modern civilian or military aircraft he was used to seeing. In fact, these planes looked like they had flown right out of World War II. Each was a distinct gray color, had a single forward propeller, a large, clear cockpit that appeared to have the pilot and one or two other crewmen behind him. All had the same distinct white star in a black circle on the underside of each wing and on the rear section of the fuselage. He also noticed each craft had the large number "19" in white on the tail. Without realizing it, he had stopped waving the signal flags as the amazement of seeing the five vintage Gruman TBM Avenger Torpedo planes overcame him.

What the hell? Josh thought. *How could these planes be here?*

The sound of the bridge radio coming to life below jolted him back from his numbness. *Voices!* He headed back down to the bridge, skipping every other rung on the ladder before he reached the deck and jerked the microphone from its holder.

Before he could say anything, an authoritative voice came though the speaker: "Vessel below, this is United States Navy Squadron 19. Are you in need of assistance, over?" He tried to suppress his excitement and took a deep breath before he responded to the call, trying not to leave anything out. With his mind racing at high speed, he had to make a concerted effort to speak slowly as he told them about his situation. He told them his name, rank, and Social Security Number first, followed by a brief description of the situation. He knew it sounded crazy, but everything he relayed was the truth, and he hoped the person on the other end didn't think he was some kind of kook.

When Josh finished, the speaker

came to life again with the same voice as before. "Cutter Tuckahoma, we have copied your transmission and will pass your info and position to a Navy PBY which is in the vicinity. We will monitor this channel if you require further assistance. Good luck, sir. Out."

Relief flooded over him as he placed the microphone back into its holder. He sat back into the Captain's chair and let out a large sigh. He didn't know what a PBY was but figured it had to be something good and decided to sit tight until he heard something further from the radio.

In just a minute or so, the radio came back to life with a new voice coming across the speaker. "Coast Guard Cutter Tuckahoma, this is Navy Trainer 49. We are approximately thirty minutes from your location. Anticipate making a controlled water splashdown on your port side and taxi to about 400 yards from you. Once positioned, we will direct an inflatable with two crewmembers to assist you for return transport. Please make all preparations needed. Over."

The young Seaman unhooked the microphone, squeezed the trigger and acknowledged the instructions. "Trainer 49, this is the Cutter Tucka-homa. Understand all. I'll be ready, sir, and thank you!"

In his excitement, Josh didn't bother to re-hook the microphone. "*All right*, time to get packing!"

Without hesitation, he made his way quickly down the steep ladder from the bridge, through the mess deck door, and down the port passageway heading aft to the berthing area to pack his sea bag. The deadness of the ship was still present, but he didn't have time to let it bother him. He had a lot to do before the rescue plane would arrive to pick him up.

In his state of excitement, Josh

temporarily forgot the combination to the lock on his rack but quickly turned the dial anyway. *"Shit, shit, shit!"* he said aloud. He slowed himself down and, more by habit than anything, rotated the mechanism to finally hit the correct sequence, pulling the lock open and removing it from the latch. He lifted the top of his rack, which was the middle of three racks stacked on top of each other, and placed the metal prop bar up, which kept the sleeping portion of his space up and open. He grabbed his folded sea bag and shook it open. He began shoving everything in sight into the green canvas bag: underwear, socks, t-shirts, uniform, jeans, etc. He had no time to sort out anything, so whatever he touched went in the bag. When he had it filled to the top and with no room for anything else, Josh hastily folded over the top flaps, placed his lock that had been on his rack into the metal loops of the sea bag, and snapped it shut.

"What else?" he said to himself, having the feeling people get when they are ready to go somewhere but sense that they must be forgetting something. *"No time for that!"* he said as he looked at his watch and found that fifteen minutes had passed like a blink of an eye. He had only another fifteen minutes before the PBY was supposed to arrive. Josh grabbed the sea bag by the shoulder strap and dragged it up the ladder from the berthing area. He'd forgotten just how heavy these things were when completely full.

He stepped out of the portside passageway hatch and headed for the fantail with his sea bag in tow when he heard the sound of aircraft engines again. But these were different from the ones he had heard before. They sounded heavier and slower.

"Must be the rescue plane," Josh reasoned as he plopped his bag down with a heavy thud. He realized that he should go to the Boatswain's Hold in the bow and get a Jacob's Ladder, a long, heavy, man-made rope and wooden ladder used to climb up or down the side of the ship.

Away he went, scampering up the main deck towards the bow and down through the opened scuttle into the hold. The compartment was just like the rest of the ship, intact but not a soul in sight. Usually, transporting the heavy ladder was a two-man job if carried intact. Because it was just him, Josh grabbed one end of the ladder and headed back up to the bow, pulling the ladder behind him. When he reached the deck, he stood up and pulled the ladder through the hole one wooden rung at a time. That was the only way he could possibly get the Jacob's Ladder up on deck.

As he finished bringing the Jacob's Ladder up from the hold, he heard a large splash off the port bow with the sound of the heavy engines increasing power then slowing. He turned and saw that the rescue plane was an old twin-engine amphibious plane from the same period as the aircraft he had seen earlier.

"Doesn't matter," Josh mumbled. "A rescue plane is a rescue plane." He waved to the sea plane as he made his way down the main deck towards the middle of the ship. As the earlier radio transmission had described, the Navy PBY Martin-Mariner sea plane taxied to a few hundred yards from the ship, and one of the side rear doors opened. A rubber raft was pushed through the opening, and two uniformed men jumped into it and began paddling in unison towards the ship.

Josh attached the Jacob's Ladder to the metal railing and heaved the remaining portion over the rail, letting it unfurl downward over the side of the ship. He then went to retrieve his sea bag and tied a long piece of rope to it as the small inflatable approached the side of the ship.

"Boy am I glad to see you guys!" he gushed as he lowered his sea bag down the side of the ship. The two men in the raft were dressed in old Navy uniforms consisting of dark blue bellbottoms with light blue denim short-sleeve shirts. Both had distinctive black double chevrons on the left sleeve, indicating they held the rank of Petty Officer Second Class. Josh noted that one of the Petty Officers had the name "Johnson" printed in black letters on his shirt above the right pocket, and the other had "Morris" on his. Both Petty Officers acknowledged his statement with nods but stayed silent. Josh climbed down the ladder and stepped into the raft, taking a seat in the middle as the two crewmen began to use their paddles to maneuver the small vessel around and begin the short trip back to the plane.

As the inflatable slowly made its way back to the plane, Josh couldn't help but turn and stare at his ship. The Tuck had been his home for almost a year. His fellow crewman were not only his friends but they were also like his family away from home. They had laughed, fought, shared their lives, their dreams, and their fears. Now they were inexplicitly gone. A sense of sadness and confusion set in as the crewman paddled on.

Josh turned back towards the plane to see a lone figure appear in the same doorway that the raft and crew had exited a few minutes before. The tall figure seemed calm and relaxed, as if this were an everyday occurrence. Then another figure appeared behind the first. Josh couldn't make out the facial features of either one of them but could see that the first man was apparently an officer, recognizing the shiny silver collar devices reflecting the sunlight.

The second figure appeared to be an older man in shorts and a Hawaiian shirt and baseball cap. As the crewman paddled toward the plane, he suddenly felt an odd sense of familiarity with the figures

Josh could sense the blood drain from his face, and shock overwhelmed him as the raft reached the side of the plane. He stared in disbelief up and into the eyes of the Navy officer that he now recognized.

"It can't be ..." Josh mumbled.

He sat motionless in the raft, stunned by who he was looking at. Looking not a day older than all those years ago on the pier at the Naval Station, the officer knelt down and smiled. The older man behind placed a hand on the shoulder of the officer and said, "Well, what are you waiting for, Lieutenant? Help my grandson climb aboard!"

With that, Lieutenant David

Hartman reached out and took the arm of his offspring as Chief Petty Officer Samuel Hartman steadied him with a strong hand from behind. With the assistance of these two men who were somehow his own flesh and blood, Josh stepped up onto the opening of the plane, still speechless as he looked into the eyes of his past.

"Welcome aboard, son," David Hartman said. "We've been expecting you."

Epilogue

(Twenty years later,
October 2003)

The Naval transport ship was pitching violently in the twenty-foot seas that had seemingly come out of nowhere, taking the crew by surprise. The young crewmember bounced against the bulkhead while making his way to his billet station as a member of the Damage Control Repair Party. He started down a ladder when the ship rose unusually high and then slammed back down into the water.

The jolt caused Petty Officer J.J. Hartman to lose his grip on the ladder and fall to the deck below, striking his head and knocking him unconscious. Falling from his pocket, the sailor's wallet hit the deck and opened to a photograph he always kept with him. It was an old picture that his grandmother had given him. The picture showed the young man's grandfather, Lieutenant David Hartman, wearing Navy dress whites and holding his son, the young Petty Officer's father, Josh Hartman, when he was a toddler. Like J.J.'s great-grandfather before them, both his father and grandfather had been tragically lost at sea decades apart while they served their country.

Young J.J. ... full name, Joshua A. Hartman, Jr. ... had joined the Navy against his mother Annie's wishes.

Even with the tragic history that came before him, he always felt it was his duty to carry on the family tradition.

Afterword

Author's note: In 2016, The former Coast Guard Cutter Tamaroa (WMEC-166) was purposely sunk off the coast of New Jersey to begin her new life as a protected reef. During my Coast Guard career, I was assigned to her for three years. I penned the following article, "Saying Goodbye to the Mighty Tam," just before the sinking for the Tamaroa's Facebook page in October 2016 in honor of her. *Family Tradition,* takes place on board the fictionalized Tuckahoma, a vessel just like the Tamaroa.

Saying Goodbye
to the Mighty Tam

She was the Coast Guard Cutter Tamaroa. What you may not know is the place she possesses in the history of our country, as well as in my personal life. "The Tam" (as we affectionately called her) was originally a Navy vessel (USS Zuni) and participated in operations during WWII in historic events in places such as Iwo Jima, the Marianas, and the Philippines before being transferred to the Coast Guard for continued service. She was the first on scene at the collision of the Andrea Doria and is perhaps most famous for her participation in the rescue of a National Guard helicopter crew as depicted in the movie, *The Perfect Storm*.

Although I was transferred off the Tam shortly before that event, I knew and still know just about every crewmember onboard at that time. This is the twenty-fifth anniversary of the actual "perfect storm" and the Tam's time has come as she will shortly be towed out to sea and sunk to become a reef. It is with a heavy heart that I, along with all who served aboard her, will say thank you and goodbye to one of the nation's grand old ladies.

I've decided to document some of my memories while onboard the Tamaroa—not for self-praise or adulation but to attempt to relay the connection a sailor and a ship forge during their time together. My connections may be more or less than others' but are powerful nonetheless. She will always be a part of me and my life.

I was assigned to the Tam as the ship's Corpsman from 1987 to 1990 and was responsible for the health and well-being of approximately eighty crewmembers. Some may not even have known my first name as I was simply, "Doc." It takes a bit of time to gain the trust of a crew, but I think I did pretty well. No matter what time of day or night, good or bad weather, on board or on liberty, everyone knew that "Doc" would be there if needed.

I learned quickly that there were times when compassion was required, and sometimes a "suck it up buttercup" was actually better. Admittedly, sometimes it sucked having to always be available, but that was my job, and I tried to do the best I could regardless of the circumstances. Treating seasickness was a fairly routine issue while underway. Some guys could take being away from the pier with no problem. Others would begin to turn green as soon as the last line was cast off.

Being underway as "Doc" could be quite boring at times but, inevitably, during each patrol, something unusual would happen that I would have to deal with. One of my favorites was the time a crewman was fishing off the fantail and had a large tri-hook get imbedded in his finger. The barb was so big that I knew I couldn't pull it out. It had to be *pushed* through his finger so I could cut the end off. The problem was that none of my medical instruments were heavy enough to cut the hook. I actually had to have pair of heavy duty cutters sent to sickbay from engineering to do the job. My patient was pretty good about the situation, laughing while I made preparations. That is—until he passed out. The hook was removed, finger bandaged up, high doses of antibiotics administered for a week or so, and he was good as new. (That's for you, Carl Boudreau.)

Berthing on the Tam was "close," to say the least. Imagine six guys in a space that had six racks, three on each side like triple bunk beds and only about two feet of floor space between. We were underway once when the

General Quarters Alarm went off in the middle of the night. (I can't remember why.) Now, when you're out in the middle of the ocean and the GQ alarm goes off, you don't waste any time. All six of us jumped out of our racks, got dressed, and were on our way to our stations in about thirty seconds—even in that cramped space. To this day, I have absolutely no idea how we did that without falling all over each other. (This one's for you, John Lucier.)

Another time, we pulled into Fort Lauderdale during a patrol for a few days of liberty, and I (along with a bunch of guys) went out one night and visited a few places to blow off some steam. You need to do that sometimes when you live in close quarters with eighty guys. I took it easy most of the time simply because I had a sense of responsibility to take care of "my" guys. Apparently one of "my" guys got into a dust-up in a bathroom with another fellow and messed him up pretty good. A couple other of "my" guys came running to me and said "Doc, you gotta get in the bathroom. Johnny got in a fight with some Navy dude, and there's blood all over the place!" My initial reaction was, "Is Johnny okay?" When told that it wasn't Johnny who was bleeding but the Navy dude, I said (and please forgive me), "I don't treat the other guys. And besides, I've got white pants on. Tell him to call *his* Corpsman!" Looking back, I probably should have checked on the battered Navy dude, and I apologize for not doing so. But my obligation was to get my shipmates the hell out of there. (I'm thinking of you, Johnny Wertz.)

During one patrol, we were directed to assist a foreign oil tanker that had an injured crewman onboard. The weather was not good at all, and we all knew this wasn't going to be fun. I gathered my equipment and joined the small boat crew for our trip over to the tanker. The seas were pretty rough at the time, and the coxswain did an amazing job of coming alongside the tanker. He had to time the rise and fall of the waves to give me a chance of grabbing the Bos'n Ladder hanging from the ship. At the top of the crest, I grabbed the ladder and put one foot on the rung. Just as I did, the wave dropped out, and there I was, hanging on for dear life with thirty pounds of equipment. Now, I just had to crawl up forty feet to get to the deck. I did, checked on the crewman, immobilized his leg, and made sure he was going to be okay. Then I reversed the adventure back to the small boat and back to the Tam. That was one time when I thought to myself, *What the hell did I just do!?* You don't think of what you're doing while you're doing it, but sometimes, afterward, you just say, "Wow!" If it wasn't for the expertise of the crew of that small boat, it could have been a very different story. (For you, Burke.)

The one medivac that I'm proudest of was during a patrol in June of 1988. The Sailing Vessel Golly Gee had become disabled during a major storm two hundred miles off the coast of New Jersey. We had to transport a female crewmember from the Golly Gee to the Tam because she had sustained a back injury. Having secured her into a stokes litter (basically a heavy wire basket), in the middle of the transfer, a wave pushed the small boat away from the Golly Gee. The stokes litter was literally hanging over the side, crewmember secured inside and scared to death, with me and the Chief Boatswain Mate the only thing keeping her from going into the sea. We struggled to hang on until the small boat was able to get back to us, and the crew was able to grab the other end of the litter and pull her onboard with them. Because the stokes litter took up so much room in the small boat, the BMC and I had to stay onboard the Golly Gee while the small boat went back to the Tam. The decision was made to tow the sailboat, so I got a really quick lesson from the BMC in how to hook up a tow line. You never know how small you really are in the ocean until you're on a floundering sailboat (or a small boat), and the waves are so big that you lose sight of your ship when you're in the trough, and all you see around and above you is thirty to forty feet of water. I was never so happy to get back onboard that old girl as I was that day. In the end, the young woman was okay, the Golly Gee got towed to safety, and I had an experience I will never forget.

These are just a few stories of my time on the Tam with perhaps the greatest crew ever. Yep, I'm biased. That's strictly my opinion, and I'll never change it. The Tam was our home, our savior, our strength, our weakness. No matter what, she always managed to get us home and deliver us to those who needed help. There are many that may not be alive today if it not for her. She will forever be a part of me. In my mind, I can still walk every inch of the old girl: the berthing area, the head (bathrooms), ship's store, mess deck, sickbay, Chief's Quarters, Bos'n Hole, dry stores, etc. You name it, I can remember it. The sunrises, the sunsets, the gentle winds, and the ungodly storms. All part of one of the best times of my life.

Perhaps it is only fitting that in a short time, she will be towed out and sunk into the very ocean that she protected us from. Unfortunately, I won't be able to attend the event and say goodbye.

Some ships are just a mass of steel, pipes, wood, and other materials used to get from one place to another with no character and no place in a sailor's soul. Others, like the Tamaroa, have forged their place in history, protected us, and have a deep connection with the sailors that served aboard her. As she slips below the surface and settles down to her final resting place, I wonder if she will know that a piece of each and every crewmember will be with her.

To some she was just an old boat whose time has come. To others, like me, she will always be ... *The Mighty Tam!*

About the Author

Herm Rawlings grew up in Hynd-man, Pennsylvania, graduating from high school in 1979. He enlisted in the United States Coast Guard the same year. He retired in 1999 at the rank of Chief Petty Officer, Hospital Corpsman. He married his wife Kim in 1984 while stationed at Group Eastern Shore in Chincoteague, Virginia. He and Kim have one son, Traise, who was born in 1987 while the family was stationed at the Coast Guard Air Station in Sacra-mento, California. During his career,

Herm and his family lived in multiple locations, such as Cape Hatteras, North Carolina; Yorktown, Virginia; Governors Island, New York; and Norfolk, Virginia. He also served aboard two Coast Guard Cutters, the Cherokee, ported in Little Creek, Virginia, and the Tamaroa, ported in Portsmouth, New Hampshire.

Following his retirement from the Coast Guard after twenty years, Herm and his family returned to the Chincoteague area on the Eastern Shore of Virginia. He re-entered government service in 2001 when he accepted his current position as the Navy Installation Housing Director for the Surface Combat Systems Center, located at Wallops Island, Virginia.

In the mid-2000s, Herm became "The Good Doctor," as the host of a popular afternoon radio show on WCTG in Chincoteague. After five years on the radio, Herm was half of the *Herm and*

Rayce Show, the first internet-based live audio/video stream show on the Eastern Shore. He also created an internet solo project, *TerraRadioOnline*, that ran for two years.

Herm has always enjoyed writing and has had multiple pieces published in local periodicals, including as an active contributor to *Shore Secrets Magazine*.

Family Tradition is his first book.

Made in the USA
Middletown, DE
29 October 2023

41462910R00060